F647

FR

Go

Writt ith

For Jim, John, Alex, Anna, Brian, Sheila

Published by Evans Brothers Limited
2A Portman Mansions, Chiltern Street
London W1M 1LE

© Duncan Smith 1989

First published 1989
Printed in Hong Kong by Wing King Tong Co Ltd

ISBN 0 237 51125 8

Louise and Fred were on holiday in France.
They were staying with Uncle Pierre, Aunt
Daisy and Cousin Jean-Paul.

"We're going to show you and Fred round Paris," said Aunt Daisy to Louise. "Our first stop will be the Eiffel Tower."

A lift carried them to the top of the tower where they could see all of Paris! Later they had lunch at a café where the tables and chairs were outside on the pavement.

After lunch they watched acrobats and clowns outside a big, colourful building. "It looks like a giant ship," thought Fred.

Then Louise began to feel very sleepy. Uncle Pierre picked her and Fred up and carried them to the underground train called the Métro. It was time to go home.

The station was very crowded and when the train arrived everyone rushed to get on. No one noticed as Fred fell with a thump on the platform. "Help!" gasped Fred as he saw the doors slide shut and the train rumble off. "Oh dear! What **shall** I do now?"

"Psssst! Monsieur!" whispered a voice through a hole in the wall behind Fred. "Come with me, I'll get you home safely." All Fred could see were two beady eyes gleaming in the darkness as he squeezed through the hole.

"How kind of you sir, to help a visitor to your city!" said Fred, bowing politely. "Oh yes!" scoffed the voice. "**Very** kind of me! My name is Finque, by the way, **Rat** Finque. Get him, boys!" Out of the darkness jumped three big rats who tied Fred up from head to toe!

They carried Fred through long, dark winding tunnels. All he could hear was water dripping, and the distant rumble of trains. Suddenly, there was a bright light up ahead. "Welcome to your new home!" hissed Rat Finque, as he untied Fred.

All around, Fred could see toys — big and small,

old and new. They were all **very** unhappy.

"What's this? Where did all of these toys come from?" cried Fred. "Same place you did, teddy bear!" snarled Rat Finque. "They were left behind because no one wanted them. Now get to work, there's my rat castle to be built!" And with that, he shoved Fred towards the other toys.

15

Françoise the tiger and a kangaroo called Mel helped Fred to his feet. "Bonjour, little bear!" smiled Françoise. "It's so sad you've been abandoned like us, but if you work hard you'll soon forget your old life." "But I **wasn't** abandoned!" cried Fred. "I'm just lost!" Mel gave a little hop. "Yes, mate, that's what **we** thought, until Rat Finque told us a different story!" Just then Rat Finque cracked a whip and yelled, "Back to work you 'orrible toys!"

17

"Better do as he says, everyone," whispered a big green space-monster. "I won't!" said Fred, stamping his foot. "Louise will be wondering where I am! And **your** friends will be worried about **you**!" "Do you really think so?" murmured a sad voice. "Yes!" called Mel. "Fred's right! They **will** be worried! We must get out of here!" A loud cheer went up and all the toys began to push and pull at the stones of the castle walls.

"Back to work!" yelled Rat Finque, with another crack of his whip. But the toys just squeaked and growled, and rumbled and roared. "You can't stop **all** of us, Rat Finque!" shouted Fred as the castle walls tumbled down. "What shall we do, Boss?" cried a fat rat. But Rat Finque had already scurried down a hole with a cry of, "Abandon ship! Every rat for himself!" The toys cheered as the other rats ran away.

21

Then the toys hurried through the tunnels back to the hole in the wall. Just as the last toy had squeezed through, they heard footsteps. ''Ooh la la!'' said a kind voice. It was a train driver. As soon as she saw the toys she picked them up and carried them straight to the Lost Property Office.

23

Next morning, when the Lost Property Office opened, the toys watched eagerly as lots of little girls and boys rushed in. ''Ah, there's Louise,'' thought Fred happily. ''I knew she'd find me!'' And by the end of the day **all** the lost toys were safely back with their little friends!